The Toy Sh

A Romantic Story of Lincoln the Man

Margarita Spalding Gerry

Alpha Editions

This edition published in 2024

ISBN : 9789357968874

Design and Setting By
Alpha Editions
www.alphaedis.com
Email - info@alphaedis.com

As per information held with us this book is in Public Domain.
This book is a reproduction of an important historical work. Alpha Editions uses the best technology to reproduce historical work in the same manner it was first published to preserve its original nature. Any marks or number seen are left intentionally to preserve its true form.

Contents

THE TOY-SHOP ....- 1 -

THE TOY-SHOP

THE Man was leaving his own front door. On the steps he paused and looked sombrely back. The white pillars of the facade rose before him in stately fashion. They reminded him of the care he was evading for the moment, and he sighed. Though he shut his eyes determinedly, he knew that another grim building just beyond, the usual end of his journeying, demanded him, and he sighed again. This time there was something more than weariness in the sound.

From around the corner of the house, which almost hid from view the white tents of the Home Guard, ran a child. He was bright-faced, and magnificent in a miniature officer's uniform.

"Oh, papa-day!" he cried. "Never mind the curtains for my stage. You are always too busy now to see my plays, anyway—!" He interrupted himself to fling this in petulantly: "But get lots of soldiers—and one company of cavalry. I can't get him surrounded without two more companies—and six cannon!"

The child lisped so in his eagerness that no one but his father could have understood him, and his father was so lost in his gloomy thought that he did not know the child had spoken. When the expected reply did not come, the boy looked his wonder.

"Papa-day—papa-day!" he cried, giving the man a little push. "I want some soldiers!"

Startled out of his sadness, the father looked at the child.

"Soldiers? All right, son; I'm off for a walk now. I saw a shop the other day."

He walked off. It was not a beautiful street down which he turned. Even the fine width of it suggested an inflated sense of its own importance. There were some good lines in the structure at the first corner, but the building was unfinished, and drooped sadly, like an eagle without its wings. Beyond that corner the paving of the street ended. Looking at the mud, the Man wished vaguely that he had worn his boots.

He swung down the row of dingy business houses, his eye on the ragged sky-line. His ungainly strides covered the ground rapidly, even though in abstraction he stumbled over the uneven brick sidewalk. The Man's face fell again into lines of melancholy thought.

"There is no hope for it," he told himself. "I will have to sign the warrant. I can't find the shadow of an excuse. It is a clear case of desertion." His thoughts drifted to the armies facing each other in the cheerless, raw December weather—his army sodden with fogs, sullen with inaction. "The poor young fellow must be punished." The Man's heart ached with comprehension. He understood so well the wave of homesickness, for which he had the more tender sympathy because of the absence of it in his own cheerless boyhood. "After all, he is a soldier, and he must be punished for the good of the others. And that boy—like so many other boys—would have been a hero, not a deserter, at another turn of the wheel. It is idleness that makes traitors of them. Where can I find a man who will end all this?"

He passed the comfortable portico of a church which carried with it a breath of thrifty village life. He had been there the Sunday before, and the minister had prayed for peace. "Peace!" The word smote him, for he had ordained war. "Peace! How can I compass it? Somewhere in the Eternal Consciousness must rest the knowledge. But how can I discover it? 'Such knowledge is too high; I cannot attain to it,'" groaned the Man.

With the thought he raised his eyes. He was opposite a young ladies' boarding-school. It was a decorous place, sedately retired on a terrace. A group of young women in billowing crinolines were returning from the daily walk. There was a lively ripple of subdued comment as he looked up.

"Did you ever see such awkwardness?" asked of her companion a girl from Virginia. "And the creases in his coat!" There was much mirth, in the midst of which a young lady from Maryland laughed out:

"Did you ever see him try to bow to a lady?"

Quite ignorant of these girlish strictures, the Man caught the eye of the youngest boarder, who, kept in the house with a sore throat, was flattening her nose hopelessly against the window-pane. Something in the face of the sad-looking man made her throw him a shy little appeal for sympathy from two red and swollen eyes. He answered it. Then:

"That child, too, I may have made fatherless even now," he thought, and shuddered.

"How to end it?" His mind kept him remorselessly at work. "I have failed. Another man might know—so many claim to know. If a better man were in my place, perhaps he could stop the killing and the sorrow."

He was approaching a poorer part of the city, where modest homes and small industries bound about the lives of simple folk, quite apart from the square, dignified old houses where the aristocrats lived. The houses seemed to press in upon him like the sorrows of the world. He thought of those who had gone out from them.

"My hand sent them out—the bright youth, North and South—to kill and to be killed. And my hand cannot bring them back. Had I the right to do it? How could I have thought that any good could come from such as I? I thought I saw clearly—I, sprung out of such darkness—having seen such sin. What right had I to think that I could lead? It was a crime!"

He came to a group of tiny two-story shops—cobblers' rooms, dingy groceries.

"Would it not be less a sin to end it all—to make way for some man who was not cursed before he was born? Surely it would not be a sin to lay it all down—no matter the way—to end it all—to make way—"

A little child, turning to go into one of the shops, brushed lightly against him, and he started. When he looked up his face was tragic. Through the daze came a recollection. Surely it was here, the fifth door from the corner, that he was going. It was a toy-shop he was looking for. Yes, that was the name—Schotz. For the son had said he wanted toys. The father entered the shop, though he saw but dimly. His mind was turned in on its own sorrows, and he went in, muttering to his own ears: "To end it all—to make way."

He had to wait for a moment while the mite who had ushered him in made a purchase. It was a girl child. She was too awe-struck by the glories laid before her to talk; but she managed to point with a fat forefinger to the penny doll she desired. The gesture with which she seized it brought—strangely enough—a smile to the deep-set eyes of the stranger who stood watching her. His face was quite different when he smiled. Lines which had seemed nothing but deep-graven channels for sorrow became paths for tenderness. Outside he heard her break into excited, high-voiced triumph, which was mingled with the chatter of her mates.

The little shop was a modest place. On one side was a counter where, safe under glass, were home-made candies and cakes, with a rosy-cheeked apple or two. But, lining the walls, tumbling over shelves, crowded into old-fashioned presses, were the toys. There were dolls, of course, patrician wax dolls with delicate eyebrows of real hair, hearty, wooden-jointed dolls that were a real comfort to little mothers. There were wheels of fortune where one could see a steeple-chase if he spun hard enough to make the horses vault the hurdles. There was a fascinating confusion of supplejacks, house furniture, houses of Oriental magnificence, little imported German toys—horses, trees, dogs. As the Man's melancholy eyes comprehended all that the place contained to minister to childish delight, something of the bitterness left them. In its place was a curious inertness. One would have said that the man's being was paralyzed with doubt.

The next instant he had seen something that brought grief back again—something that reminded him of his burden. For, marching valiantly over the shelves, storming wooden boxes flanked with cannon, were toy soldiers. There were, too, all the necessary trappings of combat—swords, guns, soldier suits, arrayed in which youthful generals could marshal their forces and sweep the enemy's army before them—while their fathers elsewhere learned the tragedy of war.

Behind the counter was a pretty, young-faced woman, who looked her fifty years only from the softness sometimes brought by the records of many days. She smiled at him in friendly fashion and, unhurried, waited his request. While she reached for the toys the son had asked for, the Man, bent over the counter, fingered the dolls left lying there from the last small purchaser with clumsy, gentle fingers.

"Who makes that 'dolly' furniture?" he asked, idly. "I wish I could get any one to work for me one-half so well. Carved, too. I didn't know there were tools fine enough to make those tiny wreaths."

Mrs. Schotz shook her head at him good-humoredly.

"My man, he speak English. I—not—can." Following her gesture, the stranger saw, in the back part of the shop, a patient figure at work.

Joseph Schotz was sitting in an invalid-chair, a table littered with tools and bits of wood by his side. One leg, bandaged and swathed, rested on a cushion. His strong peasant face was seamed and drawn with pain.

The Man was beside him in an instant.

"Yes, I make the dolls' houses and carve the furniture—great work, that, for a man, sir? I used to be a cabinet-maker at Annapolis—before my leg got so bad. No, sir, I did not learn my trade there. I was apprenticed to Cadieux, who was cabinet-maker to Napoleon. Yes, the Emperor. Who else could it have been? But that was after those pigs of Russians shot me in the leg. It was their ball that brought me here," with a contemptuous glance at his bandaged leg. "I was color-bearer—you see, I was too young to go in any other way. I was sixteen when I was wounded."

The Man found himself a chair.

"Why, no, sir, it isn't much of a story. It is only that I could never stay still. I don't believe men were ever meant to. That's why it's—" He checked himself with a glance at his wife. "I was born in the Tyrol, but the name of Buonaparte pulled me to France. Why, sir, I don't know what it was, but he is the only great man I have ever known. He made you drop everything and go with him, that is all. We never stopped to ask what it was, but—he knew his soldiers, he didn't know what it was to be afraid—and where he wanted to go he went."

The Man, who had been listening thus far with sympathy, started—at these last words—into tenseness.

"Did your Napoleon never—doubt?" he asked, with rather a breathless voice.

"If he did, no one ever saw him," chuckled the cabinet-maker, indulgently. "That was why we followed him. It sounds like very little, but—if he could call me to-day, I'd jump up and hop on one leg after him."

Had Joseph Schotz not been lost in the one story that never failed to thrill him—of his shattered dreams and his hero—he would have noticed that the face of the tall man who sat before him had lapsed into hopelessness. This time there was even something desperate in the eyes. But Napoleon's color-bearer went on:

"But you see—instead of that I'm here." He glanced at his leg again with a repressed passion of bitterness, which made him in some dark way kin to the man who listened. "It was when I couldn't fight for him that I learned to carve the wreaths on the chairs at the Tuileries—after all, that was near the end.... It is never as the Emperor on his throne that I think of him—I have seen him so—or as the general on horseback; but as the soldier in his gray overcoat going about among us. He had a way of standing, sir, as if you couldn't dislodge him—that was Buonaparte."

Mrs. Schotz had gone back to the counter with the toys the stranger sought. With an irresolute effort he moved listlessly toward them. There was a whole regiment of little men in blue, and with them a gorgeous officer in gold-decked uniform waving his sword above a prancing steed. The Man laid his hand upon the toy and moved it absently into position at the head of the men. The brave general toppled spinelessly over when the great gnarled hand was removed. The woman shook her head.

"He not—can—stand," she said, in her hesitating English. "Too heavy—of the—head. This"—substituting a plain little captain with modest sword held at attention—"this stand so you—not—can—dis—lodge him."

The Man raised his head alertly as the woman echoed so unconsciously her husband's words. The movement was a quicker one than could have been expected from the languor of the whole figure. He gave a quick glance from the man to the woman and then at the toy soldiers. Then he squared his shoulders. His hand closed again upon the top-heavy little general and, half-absently, swept him aside. The plain little officer was moved into position. The officer stood. A light that was half humor and half inspiration broke upon the rugged face of the Man who bent over them both.

"No more generals on horseback," he muttered. "My man may ride when it is necessary, but he must know how to walk, too. I want one—I wonder if I know him—who 'stands so you can't dislodge him' and who 'knows his men.' Perhaps they have given me the answer to it all. Perhaps, after all, I can find him. Perhaps. And 'where he wants to go'—was that the word?" He pored over the toys. The woman went back to her knitting. The click of needles or the noise of a tool raised or laid down was the only sound heard in the shop.

"Are you buying the soldiers for your boys? It's wonderful how they take to them these days." The voice of the cabinet-maker broke the stillness. He repeated the question before the Man heard. And even then the answer was slow in coming.

"I have but one boy to buy toys for—now," said the man, at length. "The other one—that is left—is too old. And, in spite of all, the child must be made happy."

He turned again to the soldiers as if they contained the answer to some question. His eyes fell again upon the captain. He nodded as though he recognized some one. "I believe I—know," he thought, half-fearfully. "He 'stands so you can't dislodge him'—he 'doesn't know what it is to be afraid'—he 'walks about among his men'—he 'knows them.'" The man seized the officer almost fiercely and held it in his big hand.

"I will put him there. He will stand. And"—his face lit up with sudden fire—"and 'where he wants to go' he shall go, please God!"

He swept the soldiers into a heap and pushed them from him, waiting impatiently while Mrs. Schotz deftly made them up into a parcel. But when that was done he still lingered. Suddenly he turned to Joseph Schotz with a sort of desperation.

"Did he never—waver—your Napoleon—even when he watched thousands of you—even men with children—die, and die because he placed you there—bound in the shambles?"

The cabinet-maker raised his head from his work in surprise. The inexplicable agony in the face of the other man brought an unusual thoughtfulness into the peasant's face.

"I do not know"—he hesitated—"I am not sure. He must have felt—but no one ever saw him. He could not stop. There was not a moment when, if he had halted—even to pity—all the great Thing he was building would not have fallen about his ears—and carried all France down with it. No, he could not stop. If he had been of those who falter"—here Schotz shrugged his shoulders with the gesture of the Frenchmen he had fought among—"Buonaparte should not have played the game of war."

The tall man winced. He looked for a moment as if the cabinet-maker had taunted him—knowing. Then he straightened his shoulders. His face hardened into lines of steadfastness and determination. Taking up his parcel—

"Thank you," he said, with a deeper intonation than one would have expected in return for so slight a deed—"thank you," he said to Joseph Schotz, and wrung his hand with a grasp that hurt. Then he hurried out.

When they had watched the great figure out of sight—

"Who is he—that tall man? Do you know, my wife?" asked Joseph Schotz, in their own tongue.

"Some American," replied his wife, with democratic unconcern. Then when her husband continued to gaze earnestly at the door from which their guest had departed, "A sad-looking man, I think."

"Yes, he is one that carries with him the sorrows of the world. When he came into the world he had already known what it was to sorrow. Men like that must learn to laugh or they cannot live."

"What does it matter?" she said, rallying him. "He is not thy Napoleon."

"No, he is not Napoleon," replied the man, quickly, looking down at his hand, still red from the pressure of the bony fingers. "No—Napoleon never played—with toys."

Joseph Schotz was weaker in the summer heat when the Man next came to the toy-shop. The wife was at market, so there was nobody in the place save

Joseph and the little neighbor girl who was being taught to take in pennies like a woman grown. She was not an altogether profitable clerk, however, for she outdid Mrs. Schotz in giving too good measure for the pennies. But there was need for her help, and soon there would be—more.

The Man entered the shop eagerly. From his remembering glance that comprehended the place to its farthest shelf one would have said that he had just left it. He was stooping and careworn, but his eyes sought the toys with expectation. And as he dwelt upon this spot which ministered to pure delight—a territory consecrated to those flowerings of grown-up fancy which the children call toys—his bent shoulders straightened and his deep eyes began to smile. For a few moments he said nothing. He was like a man who was drinking great draughts of water, a parched man, new from desert sands. At last he crossed to where Joseph waited.

"I found my man," he began, with outstretched hand. Then he checked himself, realizing that Joseph could not know. In that moment he saw the ravages that suffering had wrought upon the sick man's face, and a new look came into his eyes.

"How is it with you, my friend?" he asked. His voice would have been tender had he not taken care to make it merely frank—as from one man to another who was bearing pain without words. Then Joseph saw that he was changed from the man who had sought the shop the December gone by. There was sorrow in the eyes, but there was no more despair.

"Some toy soldiers, please," the stranger said to the little girl who waited behind the counter. His tone had both firmness and purpose in it, but it had changed into mere kindness when he turned again to Joseph.

"What do you think of our new general, friend Schotz?" he asked.

"He knows how to win victories," replied Joseph, "but—"

"It is long, is it not, too long? Would your Napoleon have ended it sooner?" The glance of the deep-set eyes was keen. At last he answered the uncertainty on the peasant's face with a great sigh.

"Yes, it is long—oh, more than that," he interrupted himself to say to the little clerk—"more soldiers than that." He crossed the room to give her a gentle pat on the cheek, a caress which somehow made her feel his impatience to be at play. "We need all you can get, all you have. We must reach the end quickly, no matter how many lives it may cost. That is the only way to be merciful." He was talking now to himself. The child made round eyes, but she brought the legions out. Before they were all there the Man was back at the counter.

"Cannon, too—lots of them." His voice was absent, for he was arranging the soldiers into opposing camps. "There must be some plan which will end it. This box will do for a fort. This for another. This chap is making faces, but we'll use him, too. Into your shell, sir. It's the rampart we need." The jack-in-the-box was cut short in the midst of a horrible grimace.

"Was the boy pleased with his toys?" asked Joseph Schotz from his end of the room. His voice was wistful; he had never needed to use his skill for the delight of children of his own.

"Yes, my friend."

"Yes, there is indeed a change in the Man since his first visit," thought Joseph. The smile with which the guest looked up from his toys warmed the sick man's heart, about which a chill had been gathering.

"But he wants more. He always does." There was the purest delight in the father's face as he spoke. "Just the other day I came across an upper chamber in our house which was full of toys. They were all forgotten; but each one had made him happy for a day. That's the thing. He doesn't even have to learn his lessons from them as I do." He smiled whimsically. "I am trying to give him all the toys I—didn't have. And"—his voice died away, and he forced the words with difficulty—"he must have all that I meant to give the boy who—went away."

"You mustn't spoil him," said Schotz, after a moment, with the perfunctory morality of the childless man.

The smile broke out again. "Bless you, you can't spoil children with love. Why, my boy plays with his soldiers, but he doesn't know that war is anything but a game. I wish his father could win battles with toy soldiers and tin swords." His eyes were drawn back to the counter. The next moment he was lost to every sight and sound.

Marvellous operations were soon in progress on the counter. One set of men was intrenched behind all the boxes within sight. Advance and retreat—shifting to right and to left—both sides alert, one would have said—they seemed so under the great hands that hovered over them—the besieged army handled with the same cool intelligence—both sides manœuvred for position.

The cuckoo-clock in the corner struck eleven. The little clerk stared with mouth open at the big man who played with toys. Schotz watched him with questioning eyes as the stranger knitted shaggy brows over some problem that baffled him.

Creeping over nearer, closing in around by patient degrees, came the army marshalled by the plain little officer, with sword at attention, marching on foot at the head of his men.

"I have it!" cried the Man, in heart-felt triumph. He looked up. There was a dawning realization of his audience.

"A queer thing for an old man like me to be playing with toy soldiers," he laughed, sweeping the late combatants into an undignified heap.

"So have I seen the officers at home in the *école de guerre*. Such play would aid you were you a soldier."

The tall man shot a quick glance at Joseph, in which there was much humor and some suspicion.

"Tell me—" he began. But he did not finish his sentence. He was feverishly anxious to be gone. There was so much to be done; the child's fingers were clumsy as she wrapped up the soldiers. But he found time for a smile at the little maid and a sympathetic pressure of Joseph's hand before he crossed the threshold and was gone.

At the same moment there was a bustle at the door. Mrs. Schotz hurried in, market-basket in hand. She had not laid it down before she was at her husband's side, her anxious eyes searching his face to find how he had fared.

"Clara, the tall man has been here again."

"Yes," she said, "I met him. Do you know yet who he is?"

"I have thought that I have somewhere seen a face like that," replied Joseph, slowly. "Something made me feel—his playing with the soldiers, which yet seemed more than play—he might be in the army—he might even be an officer—and yet he had not the air. Still, they are not all drilled in schools, these officers in this war."

"But listen," said his wife, as she seated herself by him, with joy that there was something to tell that he would be glad to hear. "I have something to tell you. This morning, on my way to market, everywhere there were soldiers—dirty, lean as from hunger, faces black with powder stains. At first I was afraid—"

"But, my wife," said Joseph, indulgently, "what was there to be feared?"

"I will tell you. A crowd of soldiers came swaggering into Schmidt's. They ordered him to wait on them, and when he asked for money for the food, they shook their fists at him with ugly words, and called for all to come and take what they would. Two officers hurried up and ordered them to return to their ranks, but they laughed at the officers."

"Mutiny!" whispered Napoleon's soldier, his face pale with excitement.

"They swore oaths and said that they would fight no more battles for men who were old women and stayed at home while they sweated and bled and were starving."

"Without doubt their officers ordered them into arrest?" demanded Joseph, fiercely.

"Who was there to arrest them? The officers looked white, and I was trembling. More soldiers came into the square, until everywhere there were angry faces and bodies swaying this way and that, while the men were thinking what evil they should do. At that moment a carriage drove up at full speed. There was one man in it. He stood up; he was a tall man. A hesitating sort of shout went up from the soldiers. Then there was a great muttering, and every one rushed toward him, and some were shaking their fists.

"The man stood still. He said no word. But little by little the muttering stopped and there was silence. Then the crowd began backing away from him. There was a break in the mass, and through it I saw his face. He was smiling with—well, the way fathers look at their children that have hurt themselves because they were naughty and are yet not very bad. Still there was silence."

"He held them so?" broke in Joseph. "But then he was a great man. But who?"

"Wait. He began talking to them. I couldn't hear what he said, for all the men began crowding up around him. But one moment they laughed, and the next they were wiping their eyes with the back of their hands."

Joseph was listening with shining eyes.

"When he had driven off again the soldiers went back to their camp. Some of them looked downcast and ashamed, but most of them were just boyish and good-natured, as if they had forgotten how they felt before. One boy laughed as he passed me:

"'Say, that was a good one about the tin soldier. I felt like a toy soldier myself when he turned those eyes of his on me!'"

"Who was it?" asked Joseph Schotz, eagerly. "Have they such a man? Was it the new general? I have thought he might be such a man—to win such victories. And yet"—his face fell—"that one is a short man, and this, you said, was very tall."

"The general? No!" said Mrs. Schotz, contemptuously. "It was not the general. As he drove off, some boys shouted, 'Hurrah for the President!'"

"The President!" Joseph echoed.

"The President. And, Joseph, when I saw his face I knew him." She paused to make sure of the effect upon her petted invalid of what she had to say. "It was he who came to us to buy toy soldiers!"

She fell back triumphantly when she had fired this bolt of wonder. But Joseph was looking at her with eyes in which there was no wonder—only comprehension.

"So," he said, slowly—"so—that was the President. So Napoleon would have done."

The doctor had told Joseph that he must go to his bed. The old soldier winced. A man may be brave before bullets and yet quail before the doctor. The bed was brought down into the little kitchen back of the shop. Joseph insisted on it.

"It is that I may be able to help you tend the shop," he said. But the real reason was that he might not be banished from the children's domain. He could still see Minna and Rosa and Bennie come for their toys.

Thus it happened that one morning Joseph sat propped up in his narrow wooden bed. Mrs. Schotz bustled, with much demonstration of activity, about her work. Joseph almost wished that she would go up-stairs. He was forced to keep up an appearance of much cheerfulness—if he screwed up his face when the pain came, she wept.

"I wonder if the President will come to-day," he thought. "He said he would as soon as he got back. I want to see how he looks since the surrender. Strange that it should have been on Palm Sunday." His eyes strayed to the mantel-piece, where a spray of palm waved from a gilt vase. The wife had had it in her hand when she came in from the street with the news the day before.

"If he would come, it would be easier," thought Joseph. "He would take my hand and look deep into my eyes—it would be as if he took some of the pain away from me—into his own heart." And then, because some childishness is permitted to the sick, he moved peevishly in his bed and thumped his pillow.

Suddenly the door opened. It was the President. Still, a different President—almost a new one. His shoulders were straight and held well back. He walked with a sort of joyous impatience, as though he brushed aside palms of victory. His eyes glowed. He spoke as he entered, and his voice broke into a boyish laugh. When he looked into the room and saw Joseph, the full meaning of the change struck him and his face fell. For a moment he looked almost abashed. Then, shaking his head with decision, he strode through the shop to where the sick man lay. He took Joseph's hand with resolute happiness and held it, looking full into the other man's eyes. There was no need of words between them. A heartening and a tonic influence went from one man to the other.

"It is over, friend Schotz," he said, buoyantly. "The nightmare is over; we are awake." He paused and added, under his breath, with humble, halting reverence, "Thank God!"

"They have surrendered." Joseph Schotz raised himself on his elbows.

"It was the meeting of two great men," said the President. "Mine and the other. He's a general after our own hearts—eh, Schotz—the modest man you helped me to choose!"

The sick man's face was every minute taking on the lines of hope and manly force. The other man watched him with tender eyes, in which the pity was carefully veiled.

"Yes, we chose him well, my President," said Joseph, with almost a swagger.

"You will never know how great is my gratitude, Schotz," suggested the President, "because you can never know from what you saved me—you and the toy-shop. The day when first I came here I had fallen into a pit digged by my own nature. You showed me the way out." His eyes were on the sick man, and he chose the words that would hearten most. "It was a great service you did me—and, through me, this great land of ours."

There was a light in Joseph's eyes that had been absent for many days.

"And now it is over." The President drew a breath so great that his gaunt frame expanded. He settled into a chair near the bed with a sigh of restfulness. "The boys will come home. Their mothers will meet them. Their fathers will grip their hands. No, I will not think of those who will be missing—the time for that has passed. The children will hang about their father's neck. And they will be together." The light grew in the President's eyes, until it seemed they blazed with a love which was that of child and father in one and contained the passion and tenderness of the universal lover.

Then the President rose, shaking himself like a great spaniel and laughing from delight in living.

"There are things to be done—oh, the fight is not over. Perhaps it is only begun. But to-day is my perfect moment—the first perfect moment of my life, God knows." He paused and raised himself to his full stature—challenging his fate. "It is enough to have lived for. I am content!"

He turned to Schotz again, and his face was radiant with steadfast brightness.

"There will be a future, my friend. We are ready for it, are we not? I know the path will be clear. I have begun—the first thing to be done is to heal. Beyond that"—he paused, and his forehead contracted slightly as if from doubt—"all is in the shadow." A veil made vague the joyousness of his eyes. It seemed to Joseph that his great friend was looking upon something that he himself could not see. The face brightened—the eyes opened wide—became luminous.... The President took up his words in an altered tone. "Beyond that—I cannot see," he ended, happily.

Joseph watched him for a moment. Then, uneasy, he put out his hand and touched him timidly on the sleeve. The President smiled at him again. There seemed to be no transition, and yet—they were back again in the world where things were to be done and—borne.

"And now, friend Joseph" (the President took up again the task he had set himself in the shadowed toy-shop), "when we were in the conquered city I found a toy—" He interrupted himself to laugh. "It was the only loot I permitted myself."

Joseph stared at him with puzzled expectation.

"For, after all, toys are the only things that are worth the consideration of wise folks like you and me." He was busily extricating a package from his pocket. It was done up in many wrappings. He watched while the sick man pulled off the papers, one after another. Joseph became angry with them—they seemed endless. Then the President chuckled gleefully, for he saw the color coming into Joseph's face. At last the toy stood in Joseph's hand revealed—a little tin soldier. Joseph looked at it in wonder.

"But what—?" he began. Then, "Why, it is the old uniform—he carries the tricolor. Where did you find Napoleon's soldier, my President?"

The President watched him tenderly.

"That is my secret, friend Joseph. Does he look to you like the little color-bearer, my friend, that marched gayly out, in the sparkling sunshine? But see—he is no child—his hair is gray." He bent forward. He saw a spasm of pain contract the worn face. He saw the involuntary movement of muscles when tortured nerves cry out. He saw the stark will of the man who sternly commanded his anguish to be decent and to make no moan.

"He is a soldier, my Joseph, one of my soldiers, and in the evening he is doing the greatest deed of all." The President's voice had sunk into a cadence which was melodious with all the pain the world has known—and all the joy. He held with his own the sufferer's eyes so that he could not fail to understand.

"He is a hero—!"

The President sat with the sick man in a pregnant silence, while the color came back into the face of the man on the bed. At last there came a smile. When he was satisfied that his work was done, the President rose. For a moment his hand touched Joseph's brow as the sculptor does his clay, with that touch which is a caress.

"And now, friend Joseph, good-bye."

After he had gone, Joseph looked at the toy the President had left. He put it to his lips. He held it to his meagre chest. And thus they lay, the man and the toy, until the exultation on Joseph's face softened into perfect peace.

"Toys—toys—" So his thoughts sang themselves. "Toys. Nothing else is real. Toys of tenderness—toys of mirth—toys that sail a man back to childhood—toys that sweep a man into manhood—and beyond." He held the color-bearer passionately close. "A hero!" he said. "Thank God for the man who knows our hearts. The world is his toy-shop and men and women are his toys. He can use everybody—it makes no difference how ugly a toy may be. He loves them even when they are naughty—just like a little girl when she spanks her dolly." Joseph smiled at his own thoughts with tenderness.... "Just like the Christ who suffers us to come to Him."

"I wonder ... is it because he loves people or because he plays with them that he is so far above them?—I believe he is very far off—looking on. He is really neither smiling nor looking sad—just seeing."

The room was quiet. The pain had ceased. Joseph clasped his toy and slept.

Into the damp night air drifted suddenly a wave of sound. It startled Mrs. Schotz, who sat at work by the lamp, watching late into the night. Even as she lifted her head to listen it swelled into a distant growl of thunder, threatening, sullen. A startled voice came from her husband's bed asking what the noise might be. Before she had time to answer, the door burst open, and their neighbor, the cobbler's wife, ran into the shop.

"Have you heard," she shrieked—"have you heard? They have killed him, the good President!" With the last word she was out of the door.

Joseph fell back and lay still. His hands were clinched and his lips were locked. He tried to lock his heart, too. He did not dare to feel....

"'A hero.'" he thought. "He called me that." The sound of his wife's sobbing filled the room.... No, it would never do to weep. "Ah-h!" A pang greater than he had ever known shattered him. He held that down, too. It was then that a great thought came to him—the pain taught him.

"The same future, then, for him and for me."

He lay very still while the thought grew and filled him. The sound of his wife's sobbing sank lower and lower. She crept close to her husband and laid her hand on his. He took it gently in his weak fingers, and thus they remained. The room seemed empty.

"They killed him, too, thy Napoleon," at last his wife said, timidly. Joseph started. The name of the old god made him know how far he had gone. For a moment he felt shame, as though he, too, had betrayed. Then he spoke:

"If the Emperor, too, had had—toys—and if he had played with them; if he had been able to laugh at the world and—yes—a little at himself; if he had been able to laugh at himself—and cry over other people—he would not have stayed at St. Helena. And ... he would have been almost as great as the President."

Mrs. Schotz started forward and put her face close to that of her husband. She spoke with her eyes on his eyes.

"You say—that—my Joseph?"

He nodded his head weakly but with meaning. And both were silent with that silence which follows truth proclaimed.

After a few minutes he took up his thought again.

"I thought, my wife, that the end of life had come for me when I knew that I should have to sit here in the shop the rest of the days of my life and make toys for children. Now I know that it was but the beginning. He taught me. There could be nothing greater. The toys will live in the homes of the children. They will find them, too, the toys he bought for his boy—after he has gone. But not every one will know the work that they have done. Nor will all the toys the President left be so easily discovered.... I, too, am his toy."

He stopped, for he was weak. After a time, when he had lain gazing at the wall with a look that was new to his face, an eager look that made his wife break into hopeless but silent sobbing, he said:

"It is enough to have made him smile."

When the President had been carried to his rest it came to pass that men whom the dead man had not known were called into the house to make ready for those who were to come. Through the long hours of the day they toiled. The garments that the President had worn and those things which he had used in his labor were placed aside. When it was evening they came upon an upper chamber full of toys. The men closed the door hastily and came away. But at night when they drew near to their own homes they kissed more tenderly the children who ran to meet them from their open doors.

Milton Keynes UK
Ingram Content Group UK Ltd.
UKHW010759110624
444053UK00004B/344